Hercul Superhero

Written by Diane Redmond
Illustrated by Chris Mould

Collins

CHARACTERS

- Narrator
- Hercules
- King
- Hermes, Messenger of the Gods
- Villager
- Atlas
- Hades, King of the Underworld
- Hydra
- Cerberus
- Lion of Nemea
- Cretan Bull
- Four Mares of Diomedes

SCENE 1. THE ROYAL PALACE

NARRATOR: Hercules was the son of Zeus, the greatest of the Greek gods. He wanted to prove he was the strongest and bravest man in the world.

HERMES: Your majesty, Hercules wishes to speak to you.

HERCULES: *(thumping his chest)* I'm not scared of anything! Give me the hardest labour in the world to do. The tougher the better.

KING: Can you kill a lion?

HERCULES: In a blink.

KING: Brave words, Hercules. Go and kill the Lion of Nemea …

HERCULES: No worries!

KING: … and bring me back its skin!

NARRATOR: Hercules picked up his sword and his net, and swaggered off to do his first labour.

SCENE 2. THE LION'S CAVE

HERCULES: *(yelling)* Coo-eee. Is anybody home?

VILLAGER: Don't go in there! The lion's killed four men and a donkey this week.

HERCULES: *(flexing his muscles)* Well he won't kill ME! I'm the strongest and bravest man in the world.

LION: *(from inside the cave)* GRRRRRR!

VILLAGER: Oooh! I'm not staying here. *(He runs off)*

LION: GRRRRRRAGHHH! *(The lion charges at Hercules)*

NARRATOR: Hercules stabbed the lion with his sword … but the sword broke in half.

HERCULES: The lion's skin is so thick my sword can't cut through it.

NARRATOR: The lion charged again. *(The lion takes a swipe at Hercules' head)*

HERCULES: You don't frighten me, Goldilocks! Here, try this net for size. *(Hercules jumps up and throws a net over the lion)*

NARRATOR: Tangled up in Hercules' net, the lion struggled … and roared louder than ever.

LION: GRRRRRRAAAAGGHH!

HERCULES: And now to finish you off. Grrrrrrr …

NARRATOR: Hercules squeezed the lion's throat and strangled him. Then he pulled off one of the lion's sharp claws …

HERCULES: Just the thing to cut off its skin!

SCENE 3. THE ROYAL PALACE

HERMES: Your majesty, Hercules is here with, erm *(sniffs)* something very smelly!

HERCULES: Here's what's left of the Lion of Nemea, your majesty.

KING: UGH! I don't want that disgusting thing.

HERCULES: What is my second labour, lord?

KING: You must travel to Argos and get rid of the Hydra, the monster with nine heads. And take that stinking lion's skin with you!

HERCULES: *(bowing low)* I'll be back soon.

KING: *(whispers)* I hope not!

SCENE 4. THE HYDRA'S DEN

NARRATOR: Hercules tracked down the Hydra to its den. *(Hercules sits down and lights a fire)*
It wasn't long before a hideous creature with nine heads and nine wicked eyes came looking for Hercules … but Hercules was ready for it.
(Hercules lashes out with his sword)

HERCULES: Off with your heads!

HYDRA: Aieeeeeee! Aieeeeeee!

HERCULES: Take that … and that! *(He looks puzzled)* Great gods! The monster's heads are growing back. *(He looks around)*

(Hercules runs to the fire and grabs a burning torch)

NARRATOR: Hercules wasn't just strong, he was clever too. With his sword in one hand and the torch in the other, he cut off the Hydra's heads then burned the stumps so that the heads could not grow back.

HYDRA: Aieeeeeee!

HERCULES: Well, that's another labour done. I'll take the Hydra's body back to the King to prove how brave and strong I am.

SCENE 5. THE ROYAL PALACE

HERMES: Hercules is back again, your majesty. The smell's even worse this time.

(Hercules enters carrying the dead Hydra)

KING: I don't want that thing – take it away!

HERCULES: Your majesty, give me something even harder to do.

KING: I don't want you to *kill* anything this time, Hercules – I want you to do some cleaning.

HERCULES: *(insulted)* Heroes don't clean!

KING: This is no ordinary cleaning job. You must clean the stables of King Augeus in ONE DAY.

HERCULES: Humph! I asked for a hard labour, but you give me an easy one.

KING: *(laughing)* Ha ha ha! Wait till you see the stables, Hercules.

(Hercules leaves grumpily)

SCENE 6. THE STABLES

NARRATOR: King Augeus kept a thousand cattle in his stables. The stables had NEVER been mucked out and they stank.

HERCULES: UGH! The muck must be over two metres high! How can I get rid of all that in ONE DAY?!
(He looks around)

(Sound effects: GLUG GLUG GLUG)

HERCULES: There's a fast flowing river behind the stables. That could be very useful. First I'll move the cattle from the stables … *(Hercules shoos the cattle out of the stables, then runs to the river and starts moving heavy boulders)*

HERCULES: Then I'll make a dam across this river.

(Sound effects: GLUG GLUG GLUG)

NARRATOR: Hercules made the river flow through the stables and – WHOOOSH! – the stables were clean for the first time in ten years.

HERCULES: *(laughing)* Ha ha! That's got rid of that lot!

SCENE 7. THE ROYAL PALACE

HERMES: I'm so sorry, your majesty, but there's a man to see you and he's covered in muck!

HERCULES: I'm back, your majesty. I cleaned up the stables – they're spotless now.

KING: *(whispering)* POOH! I wish he'd cleaned himself up too!

HERCULES: What's my fourth labour, lord?

KING: Hercules, you must do the impossible. You must go to Crete and catch the fire-breathing bull!

HERCULES: A bull! No problem! *(He swaggers off)*

SCENE 8. CRETE

NARRATOR: In Crete, a wild bull terrified the people so much that nobody would leave their homes. When Hercules saw the bull with fire blazing from its nostrils, he couldn't believe his eyes.

(Hercules and the fire-breathing bull face each other)

HERCULES: What a WHOPPER!

BULL: *(bellowing)* Moooooooo!

NARRATOR: The bull dropped his head and charged at Hercules.

BULL: *(still bellowing)* Moooooooo!

(Hercules skips sideways and the bull misses him)

HERCULES: Aha – fooled you!

NARRATOR: The bull charged again.

(Hercules runs behind the bull and grabs its horns)

HERCULES: *(groaning with effort)* Ahhhhh!

NARRATOR: Hercules used his huge strength to drag the bull to its knees. The bull was too tired to fight any more.

(Hercules ties up the bull's feet)

HERCULES: Phew! That was a tough one. Let's see what the King has to say about you, big boy!

SCENE 9. THE PALACE

HERMES: Your majesty, Hercules is back again … and he's not alone!

(The King runs behind his throne to hide)

KING: Get that monster out of here!

BULL: *(bellowing)* Moooooooo!

HERCULES: But I carried him all the way here so that you could see how big he is.

KING: I don't want to see him – I want him to GO AWAY!

HERCULES: What is my fifth labour, your majesty?

KING: Your next labour is harder than any before. You must go and tame the Mares of Diomedes.

HERCULES: Oh good. I love horses. I'll be able to ride back when I've tamed them.

SCENE 10. DIOMEDES' STABLE

NARRATOR: Diomedes had four powerful horses that pulled his racing chariot. They ate nothing but human flesh.

(Hercules looks at the mares whose heads peer over the stable door)

MARES: *(hungrily)* NEIGH! NEIGH! NEIGH! NEIGH!

HERCULES: Maybe I'll talk to them AFTER they've had their supper.

NARRATOR: The mares broke down the stable door and galloped off over the countryside. They ate everyone they came across – men, women and children.

MARE 1: CHOMP … CHOMP!

MARE 2: NIBBLE … NIBBLE!

MARE 3: CRUNCH … MUNCH!

MARE 4: NEIGH!! *(The mares run around the audience nibbling them!)*

NARRATOR: After the mares had eaten enough, they galloped back to their stables in a *much* better mood.

(The mares trot back to the stables where Hercules is waiting for them)

HERCULES: Here, nice horses ... come and have some sweets.

NARRATOR: Hercules held out his hand, and as each horse took a sweet he put a rope around its mouth.

HERCULES: Be good – I'm taking two of you to see the King.

SCENE 11. THE PALACE

NARRATOR: The horses were *not* good, and they were hungry again. They chased the King around the palace and tried to eat *him*!

MARES: *(wildly)* NEIGH! NEIGH!

HERMES: The King demands you take the horses away, Hercules!

(Hercules claps his hands)

NARRATOR: The two horses stopped chasing the King and trotted up to their new master.

MARES: NEIGH! NEIGH!

KING: *(fed up)* Will you *please* stop bringing monsters into my palace?

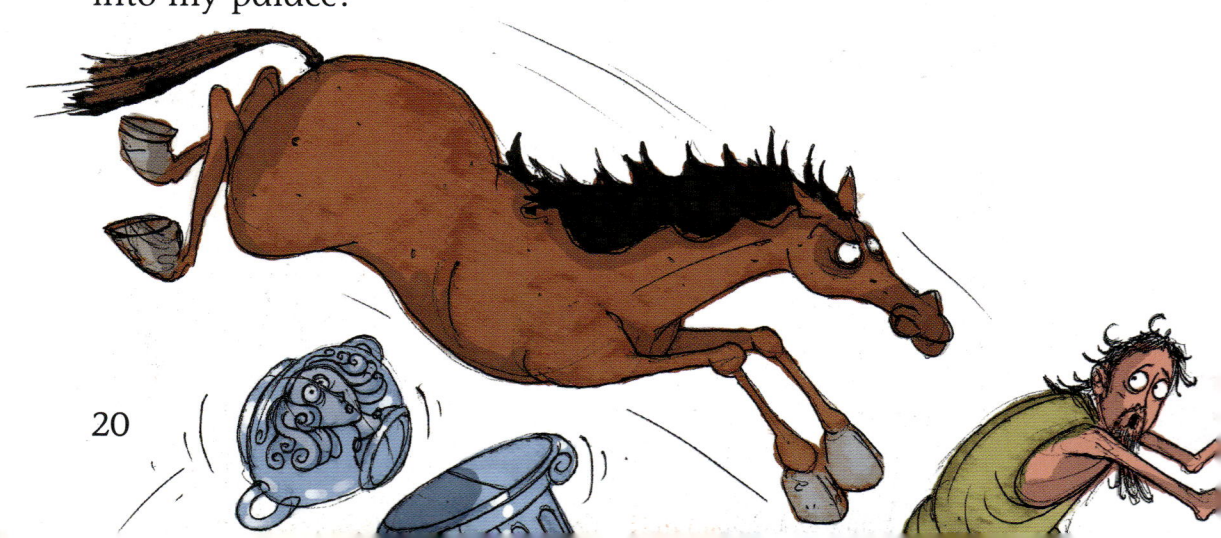

HERCULES: Sorry, lord – what is my sixth labour?

KING: I want you to pick me some apples.

HERCULES: *(insulted)* Strong men don't pick apples!

KING: These aren't any old apples, Hercules. I want the Golden Apples from the Gardens of Hesperides.

HERCULES: The Gardens of Hesperides are in Africa! The apples will be rotten by the time I get back.

KING: *(whispering)* At least apples can't bite!

SCENE 12. THE ATLAS MOUNTAINS

NARRATOR: The Gardens of Hesperides were looked after by Atlas's daughters. Hercules found Atlas in the mountains, holding the world on his shoulders.

HERCULES: Will you ask your daughters if I could have some of their Golden Apples, Atlas?

ATLAS: I'll have to go and find them. Would you mind holding the world for me while I'm away?

HERCULES: Not at all – I'm the strongest man in the world!

(Atlas places the globe on Hercules' shoulders, then he stretches)

ATLAS: Hah! What a relief! I've been holding that thing for twenty years! See you later! *(He waves and hobbles off)*

HERCULES: *(calling after him)* Don't be too long, Atlas. I may be the strongest man in the world, but the world is very heavy.

NARRATOR: Atlas was gone for a very long time.

HERCULES: *(worried)* What if he doesn't come back? I'll be stuck here for EVER.

NARRATOR: But Atlas *did* come back, and in his hands were five Golden Apples.

ATLAS: Thanks for giving me a break, Hercules. You'd better put the world back on my shoulders.
(Atlas groans, and stoops with the weight of the world back on his shoulders)

HERCULES: It's all yours, Atlas. Thanks for the apples – and good luck!

SCENE 13. THE PALACE

HERMES: Hercules has returned from Africa, your majesty. He's got some tasty apples for you.

NARRATOR: The King was *delighted* with the Golden Apples – they didn't stink, bite or chase him! He was also amazed that Hercules had done everything he'd asked.

KING: Only one more labour, and then you will have proved you are the strongest and bravest man in the world, Hercules.

HERCULES: What is my seventh labour, sir?

KING: Go to the Underworld and bring back Cerberus, the three-headed hound that guards the Gates of Hell.

HERCULES: I could be gone some time.

KING: That's the idea!

SCENE 14. THE UNDERWORLD

(King Hades is waiting at the gates of the Underworld)

NARRATOR: Hades, the King of the Underworld, had heard about Hercules' seventh labour and was not going to make things easy for him.

HADES: You *can* borrow Cerberus – but first you must catch him without using your sword or spear.

(Hercules walks towards the three-headed dog)

CERBERUS: GRRRRROWL!

HERCULES: This could be tricky! Hello, doggy. Who's a good doggy?

CERBERUS: GRRRRRROWL!

HERCULES: Come a bit closer to Uncle Hercules, Cerby.

CERBERUS: GRRRRRROWL!

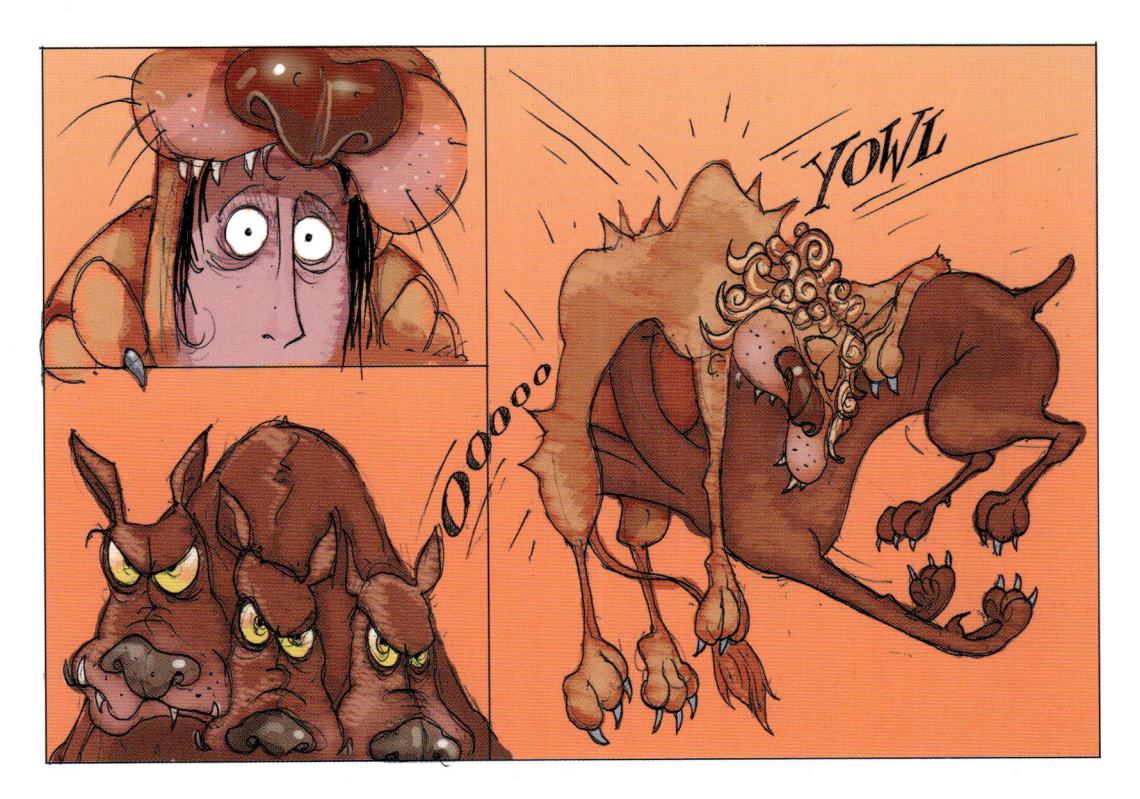

(Hercules takes the lion's skin from around his shoulders)

NARRATOR: When Cerberus was near enough, Hercules threw the lion's skin over the dog's three heads. Cerberus couldn't see a thing from any of his six eyes.

CERBERUS: *(whimpering)* Oooooo, yowl!

HERCULES: Aha! I caught him, Hades.

HADES: *(grumpily)* He's a good guard dog – don't forget to bring him back.

SCENE 15. THE PALACE

HERCULES: Come on, Cerby, let's go and see the King.

CERBERUS: RUFF! RUFF! RUFF!

HERMES: It's a mad dog, your majesty – and Hercules. He wants to say hello to you.

(Cerberus runs to the throne and grabs the King's foot. He starts to shake it, like a rag)

CERBERUS: GRRRR! GRRRR! GRRRR!

KING: AHHH! Help me, Hercules.

CERBERUS: RUFF! RUFF! RUFF!

HERCULES: *(shouting)* CERBERUS! HEEL!

(Cerberus wags his tail as he runs to Hercules)

NARRATOR: Hercules really had tamed the three-headed hound dog from hell.

HERCULES: I have finished my seven labours, lord.

KING: Yes, Hercules, you have. You really are the strongest and bravest man in the world.

HERCULES: *(patting Cerberus's three heads)* Come on, boy, now we can all go HOME!

CERBERUS: Ruff! Ruff! Ruff!

WANTED

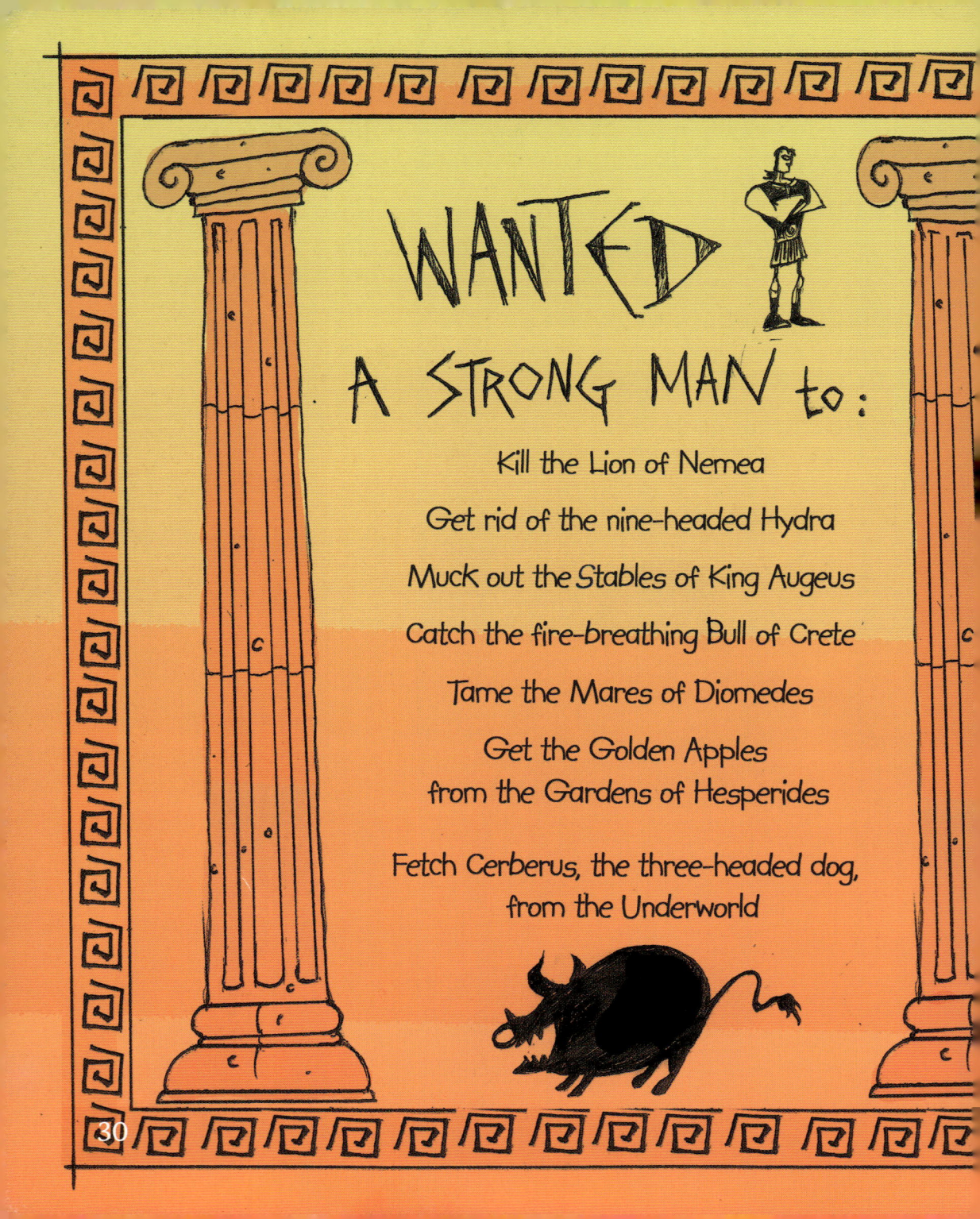

A STRONG MAN to:

Kill the Lion of Nemea

Get rid of the nine-headed Hydra

Muck out the Stables of King Augeus

Catch the fire-breathing Bull of Crete

Tame the Mares of Diomedes

Get the Golden Apples
from the Gardens of Hesperides

Fetch Cerberus, the three-headed dog,
from the Underworld

Don't apply if you don't like animals.

Don't apply if you are not brave and strong.

Do apply if your name is Hercules.

Applications to the King, the Royal Palace:

Ideas for reading

Written by Clare Dowdall, PhD
Lecturer and Primary Literacy Consultant

Reading objectives:
- discuss and clarify the meanings of words, linking new meanings to known vocabulary
- make inferences on the basis of what is being said and done
- discuss the sequence of events in books and how items of information are related

Spoken language objectives:
- participate in performances, role play and improvisations
- select and use appropriate registers for effective communication
- ask relevant questions to extend their understanding and knowledge
- use spoken language to develop understanding through speculating, hypothesising, imagining and exploring ideas

Curriculum links: Citizenship

Interest words: Hercules, labour, narrator, Underworld, Hydra, Cerberus, Nemea, Diomedes, majesty, muscles, Goldilocks, struggled, hideous, creature, Augeus, boulders, swaggered, chariot, Hesperides, Atlas

Word count: 1,801

Build a context for reading

This book can be read over two reading sessions.

- Introduce the book to the children and discuss the cover. Ask the children what they think a superhero is. Do they know of any? *What words describe a superhero?* (for example, *brave, heroic, strong, special*.)
- Read the blurb together and discuss the word 'labours'. Ask the children to infer what 'dangerous labours' means. *What sort of work do superheroes do?*
- Scan pp2–3 together and ask the children to point out the key features of a playscript. Discuss the conventions, e.g. use of stage directions, character identification, punctuation.
- Using p2, introduce the characters and help the children to read their Greek names. Allocate one colour set of characters to each child in the group (of up to six), using the colour bands on p2 and the corresponding coloured character names in the playscript.
- Rehearse reading p3. Model using an expressive, dramatic voice. Remind children to read speech and follow the stage directions.

Understand and apply reading strategies

- Ask the children to read the playscript through quietly to p8. Remind them to look out for stage directions and words that give clues about how to say the lines.